ABC T-Rex

A B C D

I J K L M

S T U V

E F G H

N O P Q R

W X Y Z

ABC T-Rex

BERNARD MOST

VOYAGER BOOKS • HARCOURT, INC.

Orlando   Austin   New York   San Diego   London

To Samantha and Nicholas with much love

Requests for permission to make copies of any part of the work should be submitted online at www.harcourt.com/contact or mailed to the following address: Permissions Department, Harcourt, Inc., 6277 Sea Harbor Drive, Orlando, Florida 32887-6777.

www.HarcourtBooks.com

First Voyager Books edition 2004
Voyager Books is a trademark of Harcourt, Inc., registered in the United States of America and/or other jurisdictions.

The Library of Congress has cataloged the hardcover edition as follows:
Most, Bernard.
ABC T-Rex/by Bernard Most.
p. cm.
Summary: A young T-Rex loves his ABCs so much that he eats them up, experiencing on each letter a word that begins with that letter.
[1. Dinosaurs—Fiction. 2. Alphabet.] I. Title.
PZ7.M8544Ab 2000
[E]—dc21 98-51128
ISBN 978-0-15-202007-1
ISBN 978-0-15-205028-3 pb

E G I K M N L J H F

The illustrations in this book were done in Pantone Tria markers on Bainbridge board 172, hot-press finish.
The display type was set in Vag Rounded Bold.
The text type was set in Vag Rounded Thin.
Color separations by Tien Wah Press, Singapore
Printed and bound by Tien Wah Press, Singapore
Production supervision by Sandra Grebenar and Pascha Gerlinger
Designed by Linda Lockowitz

There once was a T-Rex who loved his ABC's so much, he ate them up.

A w**a**s **a**ppetizing.

B was
even **b**etter.

C was chewy.

D taste**d d**elicious.

E was **e**asy to **e**at.

F was a **f**east.

G got **g**obbled up.

H made **h**im **h**ungrier.

L was luscious.

M was a mouthful.

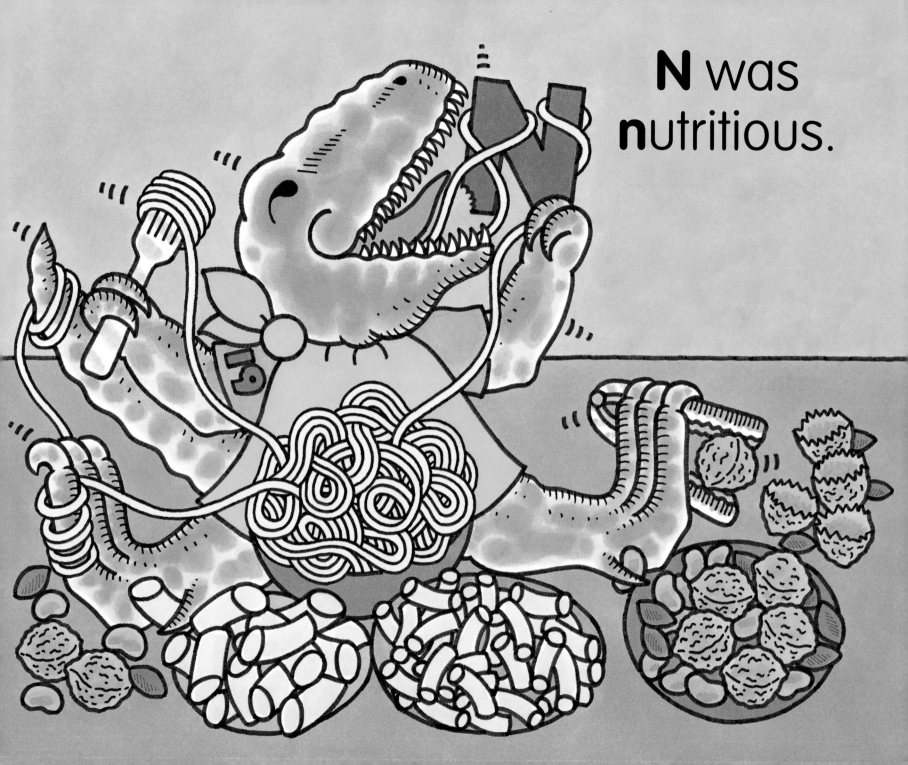

N was
nutritious.

O tasted **oh** s**o** g**oo**d.

Q was **q**uite **q**uenching.

R was
ref**r**eshing.

S wa**s** for **s**haring.

T was a t**reat**.

U upset
his t**u**mmy.

V was full of **v**itamins.

W was **w**onderful.

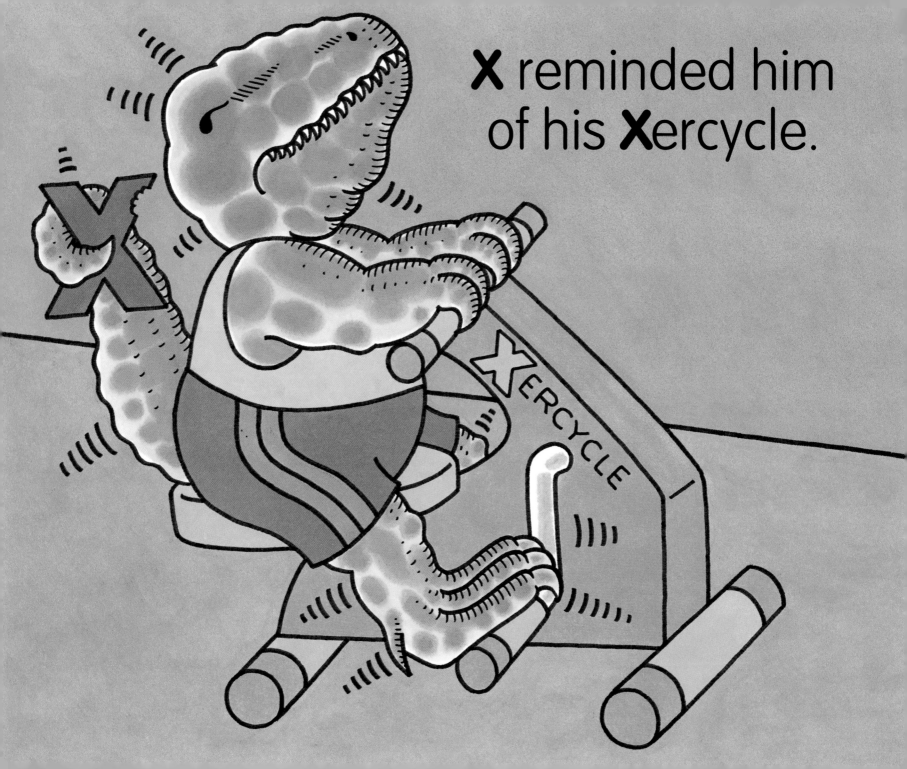

X reminded him of his **X**ercycle.

Y made him **y**awn.

Z was for **z**…**z**…**z**…**z**…**z**….

Some extra things to look for:

acorns
airplanes
ant
apple tree
arms

balls
basket
bats
bear
bed
bib
blanket
book (by Bernard)
bowl
bug
butter knife

camera
cap
cardinal
carousel
cat
caterpillar
circus tent
clouds

daisies
dinosaur
dishes
dog (dalmatian)
dog tag
dragonfly
ducks

egg cup
eggshells
electric light
elephant
eye

fence
flowers
fly
foot
football
forks
frog
frying pan

garden tool
gate
giraffes
glove
grass
grasshopper
grill

Hadrosaurus
handles
hat
hearts
hedge
hill
hippo
hooks
hose
house

ice cubes
Iguanodon
invitation

jacket
jars
jay
jeans

kangaroos
kettle
key
kitchen
kitten
knees
knife
knobs
knot

ladder
ladybug
lawn mower
leaves
leg
lizards
log

m

mamma
mammoth
mitt
moon
mug

n

napkin
numbers
nutcracker
nutshells

octopus
oven
overalls

o

pants
paper plates
park
patches
path
pen
pencil
picnic basket
pitcher
pocket
polka dots
pot
Protoceratops

p

q

quart jars
quilt

red
refrigerator
rhinoceros

r

sailboat
sand
sandals
sea
shirts
sky
spoon
Stegosaurus
straws
sun
suspenders

s

table
tails
tea bag
teapot
teaspoon
teeth
tie
tongue
toothpicks
tray
trees
T-Rex
Triceratops
T-shirt
turtle

t

umbrella
undershirt
unicorn
uniform

u

vest
vines

wagon
walrus
watch
wheelbarrow
wheels
worm

Xercycle

yogurt
yellow

zebra
Zoodles
Z-z-zoink!

a b c d

i j k l m

s t u v

e f g h

n o p q r

w x y z

Walt Chrynwski

BERNARD MOST started writing children's books to amuse his own children (who are also dinosaur aficionados). He is the author and illustrator of several books for children, including *If the Dinosaurs Came Back, Dinosaur Cousins?,* and *The Littlest Dinosaurs.* Mr. Most lives in New York with his wife.